Hidden Treasure

For
W. R. Allen

First published under the title Herbert and Harry by
Thomas Nelson Australia
Editor: Anne Bower Ingram
First American edition 1987
Printed in Singapore
First impression

Library of Congress Cataloging-in-Publication Data
Allen, Pamela.
Hidden treasure.
Originally published as: Herbert and Harry.
Summary: After claiming the treasure that he and
his brother haul out of the ocean,
Herbert spends the rest of his life fearfully
guarding it from possible thieves.
[1. Greed—Fiction]   I. Title.
PZ7.A433Hi   1987   [E]   86-22695
ISBN 0-399-21427-5

Hidden Treasure
Pamela Allen

G. P. Putnam's Sons
New York

ONCE upon a time there were two
brothers called Herbert and Harry who lived
together in the same house,

dug together in the same garden,

and fished together from the same boat.

One day while they were out fishing they hauled
up a great treasure.

"This treasure is mine," shouted Herbert, "I pulled it up."

"No!" said Harry, "I chose this place to cast our net."

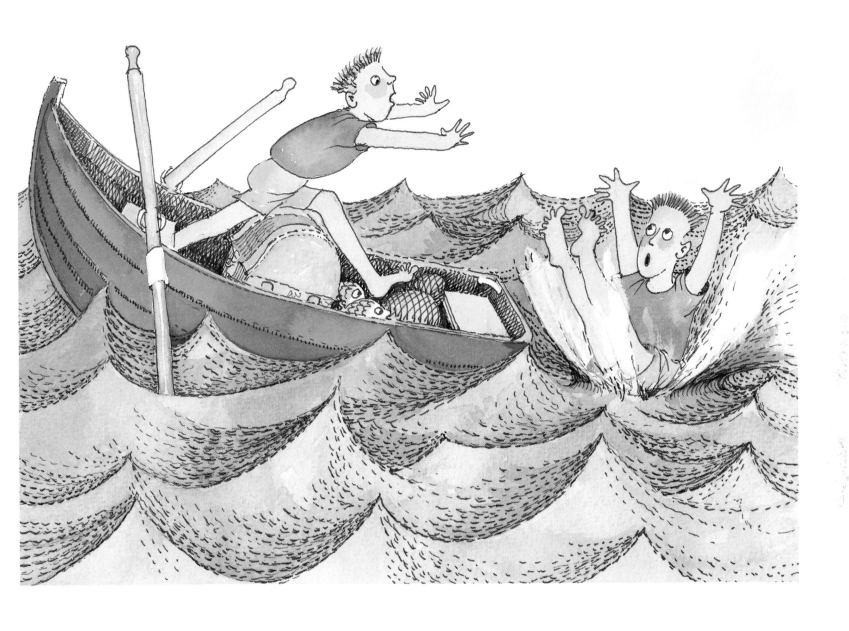

So Herbert pushed Harry and Harry fell . . . SPLASH!

Harry was a strong swimmer and
managed to get safely home.

While Herbert rowed the treasure as fast as
he could, for as long as he could, until he reached
a lonely stretch of coast.

From there he started to walk. He wanted to get
as far away from Harry as possible.

At last Herbert lay down to sleep.
But even though it was very dark, and he was
very tired, he could not sleep.

What if Harry came and stole the treasure?

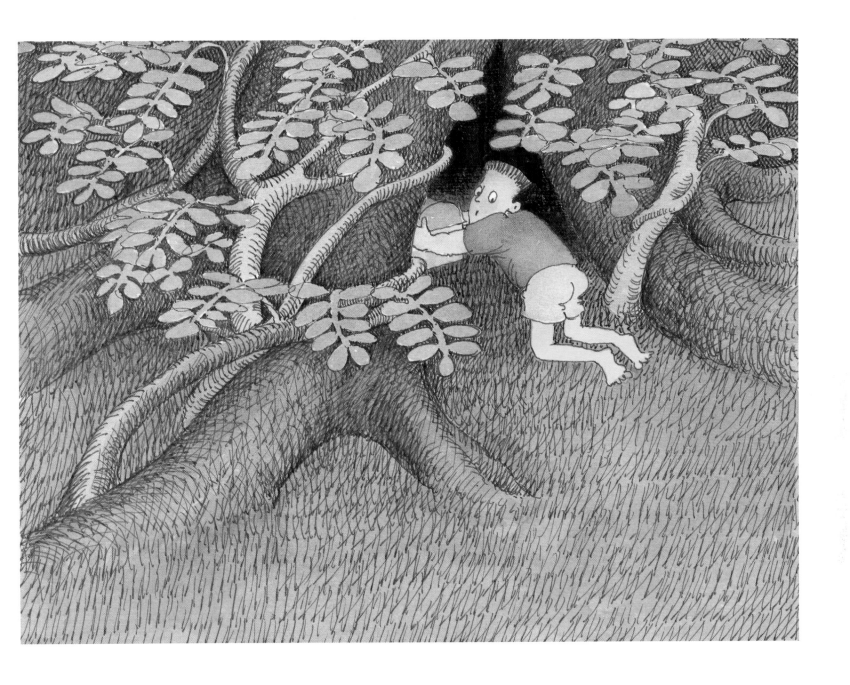

So the next day Herbert hid the treasure
among the roots of an old tree. But that night,
when it got dark, he still could not sleep.

What if someone had seen him put it there?

He decided to take the treasure high
into the hills where no one would find it.
He walked many days and many nights.
The land got emptier and emptier.

And the treasure got heavier and heavier.

At last he reached the highest mountain
in the land, and there he hid the treasure
under some rocks. But still he could not sleep.

What if someone had followed him, and stole
the treasure while he slept?

He decided the only way to keep the
treasure safe was to put it in a place which
was so strong, no one could get in.

He began to chip the rock.

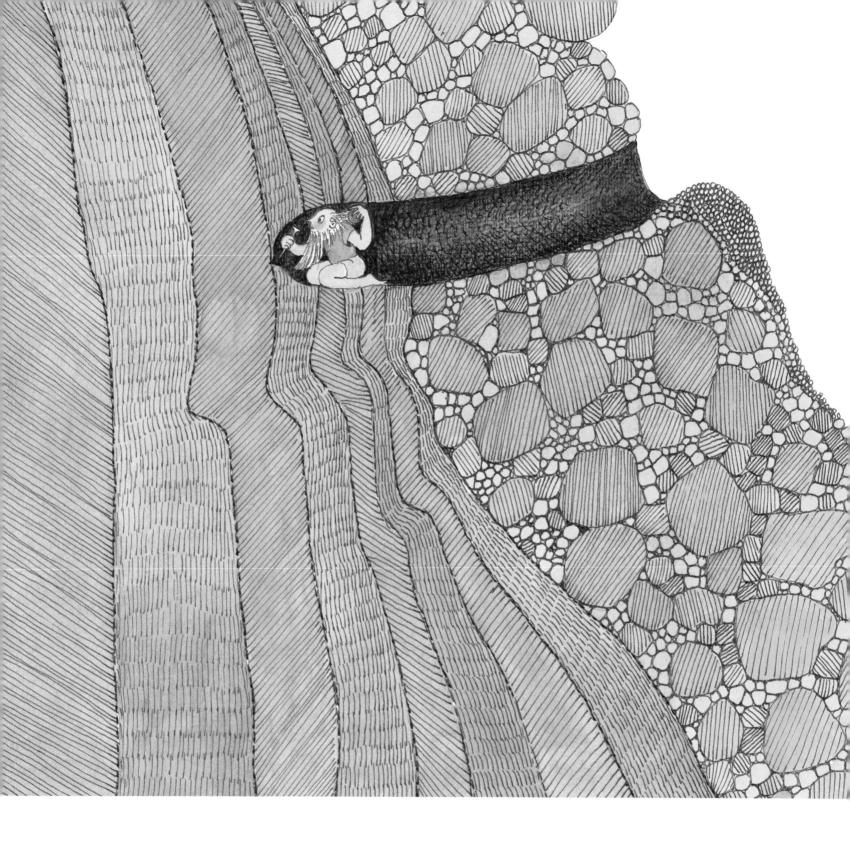

Chip chip, chip chip, chip chip,

chip chip,   chip chip, went Herbert.

Many years passed.
At last he had made a deep dark tunnel into the
middle of the tallest mountain in the land.

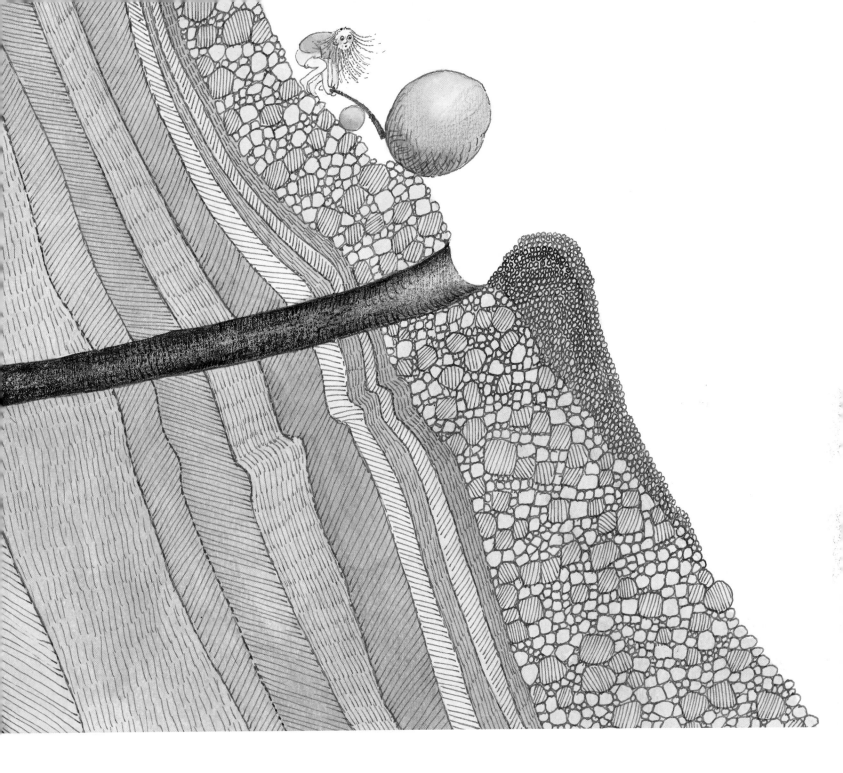

He pushed the treasure right to the end of the tunnel,
then blocked the entrance with a huge boulder.

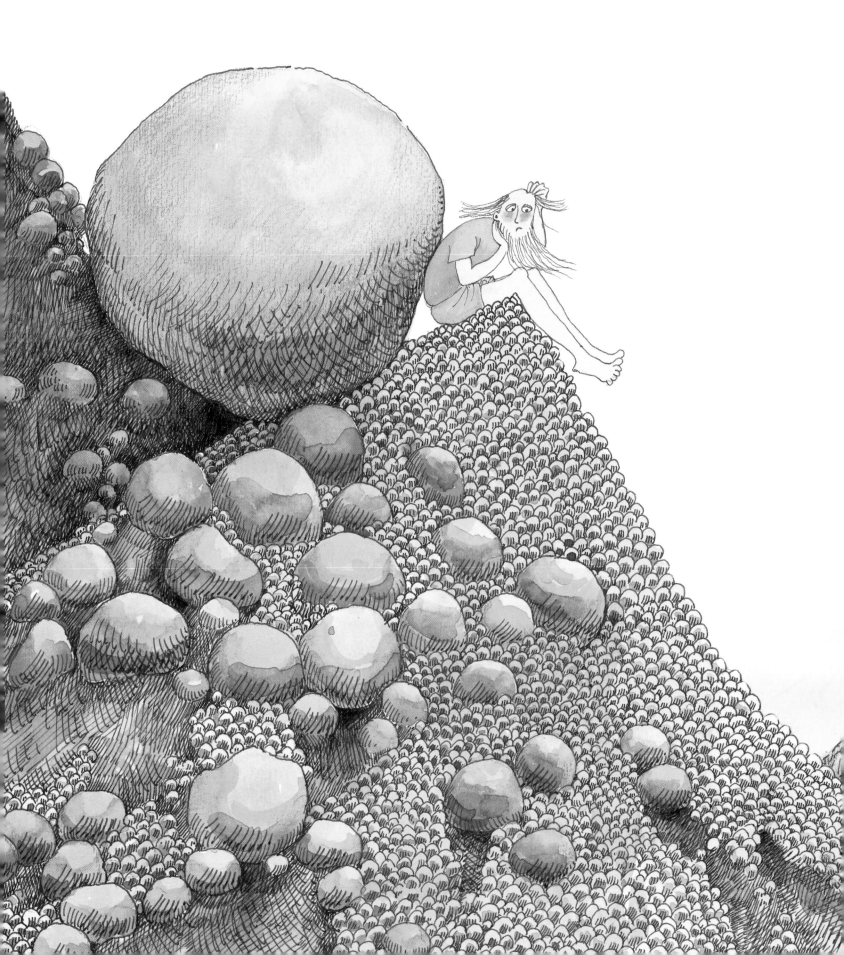

But still he could not sleep.

What if someone forced him to tell where
the treasure was? Then they could steal it.

He decided he must protect himself.

To protect himself, Herbert needed guns.

Lots of guns.

But guns were not enough.

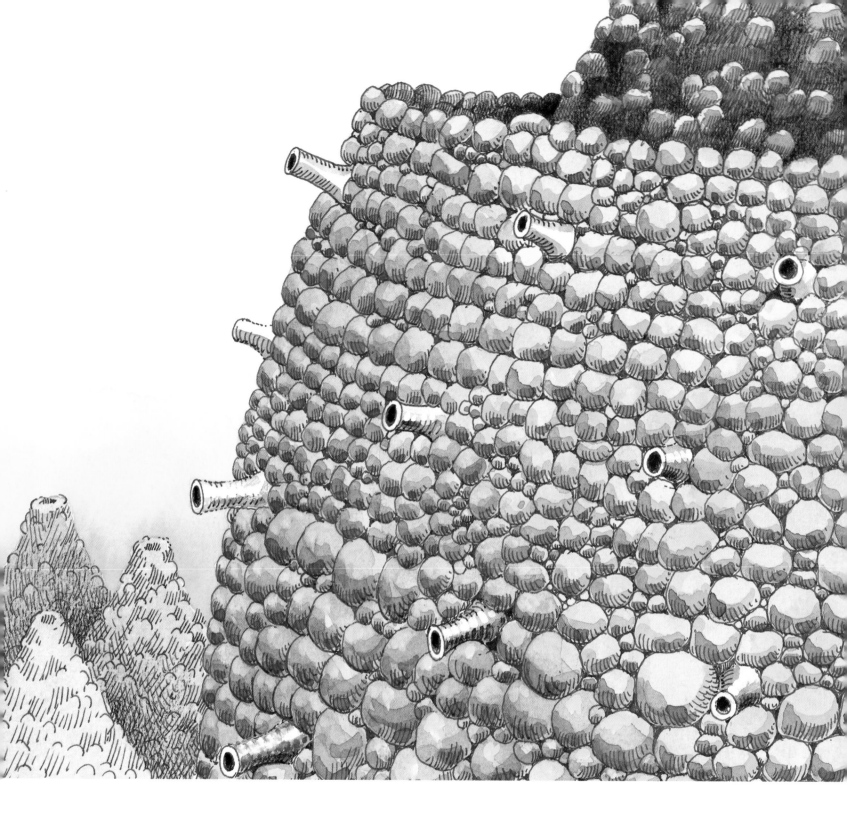

Herbert needed a fort.

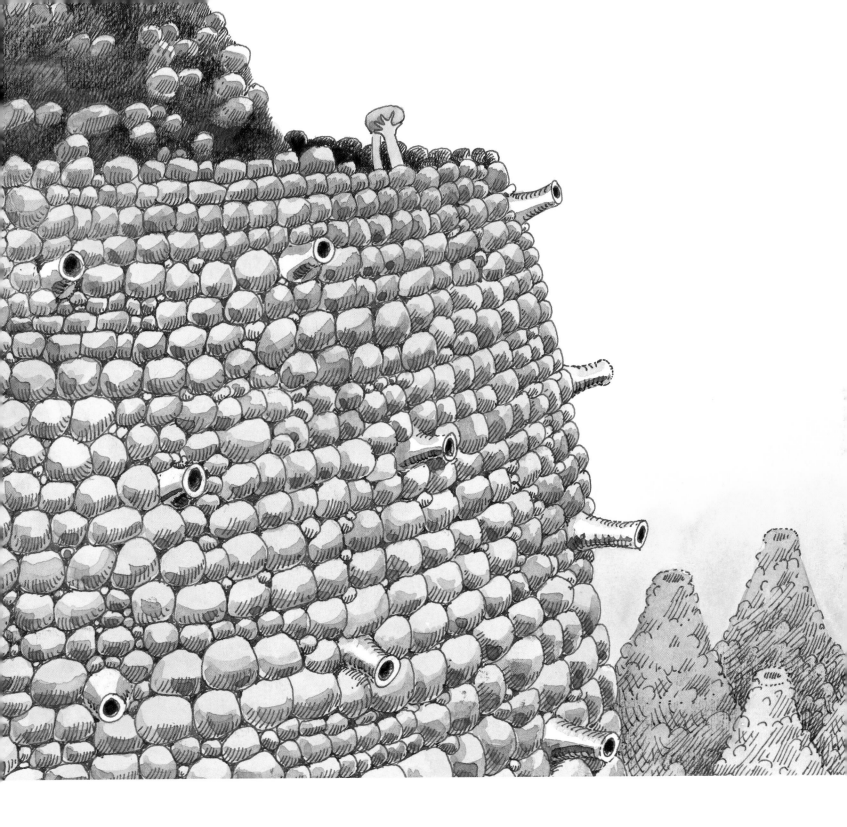

Many more years passed.

Today, Herbert and Harry are very old men.

Herbert still guards the treasure in his fort
on top of the highest mountain in the land.

But still, he cannot sleep.

While Harry, who had no treasure,
has always been able to sleep soundly.

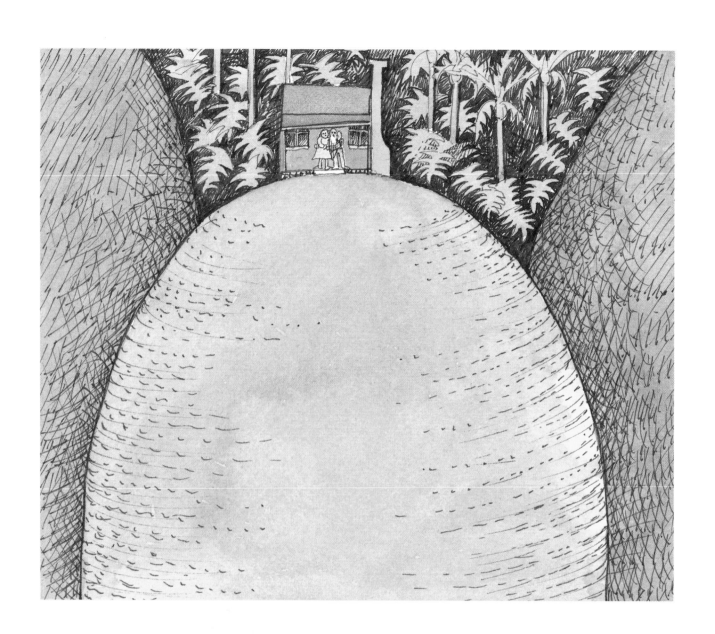